THE EENSY-WEENSY SPIDER

1. F | C7 | F
The een - sy ween - sy spi - der went up the wa - ter - spout.

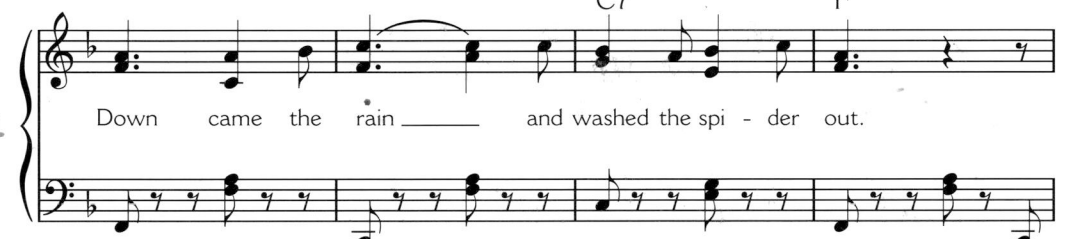

2. C7 | F
Down came the rain _____ and washed the spi - der out.

3. C7 | F
Out came the sun _____ and dried up all the rain. And the

4. C7 | F/C
een - sy ween - sy spi - der went up the spout a - gain.

You can play this simple hand-motion game when you sing "The Eensy-Weensy Spider." Just carry out the actions described below as you sing each line of the song. It's fun by yourself or with a friend!

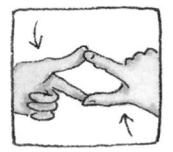 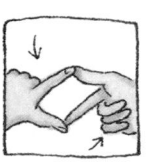  

① Place your right thumb on your left forefinger. Then twist your hands and place your left thumb on your right forefinger. Continue to swivel your hands in this climbing motion as the spider goes up, up the spout!

② Move hands up and down while you wiggle your fingers. It's raining!

 OR    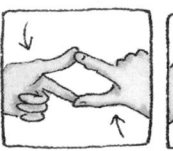

③ Make a circle with your thumbs and fore-fingers; now raise it slowly to the rhythm of the song. Or, instead, use your arms to create a large circle in the air. The sun is out!

④ Now repeat the climbing motion with your fingers and thumbs.

Teach your friends!

For three more small Cousins, Hannah and David Iafrati and Jessica Freedman—M.A.H.

Text copyright © 2000
by Mary Ann Hoberman
Illustrations copyright © 2000
by Nadine Bernard Westcott

First Edition
Library of Congress Cataloging-in-Publication Data
Hoberman, Mary Ann.
The eensy-weensy spider / adapted by Mary Ann Hoberman ;
illustrated by Nadine Bernard Westcott. — 1st ed.
p.   cm.
Summary: An expanded version of the familiar children's finger-play rhyme
describing what the little spider does after being washed out of the waterspout.
ISBN 0-316-36330-8
1. Children's songs — United States Texts. [1. Spiders Songs and music. 2. Songs.]
I. Westcott, Nadine Bernard, ill. II. Title.
PZ8.3. H66Ee 2000
782.42164'0268 — dc21
[E]   99-25701

10 9 8 7 6 5 4 3 2 1
TWP
Printed in Singapore
The illustrations for this book were done in watercolors
and ink. The text was set in Cantoria, and the
display type is handlettered.

For Willy, Becky and Wendy—N.B.W.

THE EENSY-WEENSY SPIDER

adapted by MARY ANN HOBERMAN

illustrated by NADINE BERNARD WESTCOTT

LITTLE, BROWN and COMPANY

BOSTON   NEW YORK   LONDON

The eensy-weensy spider went up the waterspout.
Down came the rain and washed the spider out.
Out came the sun and dried up all the rain.
And the eensy-weensy spider went up the spout again.

The eensy-weensy spider got up one day in spring.
She stretched out all her legs and she began to sing.
"La!" sang the spider. "It's such a lovely day!"
And the eensy-weensy spider went skipping out to play.

The eensy-weensy spider met a baby bug.

"Hi!" said the spider and gave the bug a hug.

"Ugh!" said the bug. "Your hug is much too tight!"

"I'm sorry," said the spider. "I meant to be polite."

The eensy-weensy spider walked down the garden path.
Down came the rain and gave her quite a bath.
Out came the sun and dried her dry as chalk.
And the eensy-weensy spider continued on her walk.

The eensy-weensy spider went swimming to get cool.
"Out!" croaked the frog. "No spiders in my pool!"
"Please!" begged the spider. "I'd really like to swim."
So the frog allowed the spider to swim along with him.

MARCH!

The eensy-weensy spider was in a big parade.
Boom! banged the drums. The trumpets loudly played.
"March!" roared the leader. "Just listen to the beat!"
But the eensy-weensy spider kept tripping on her feet.

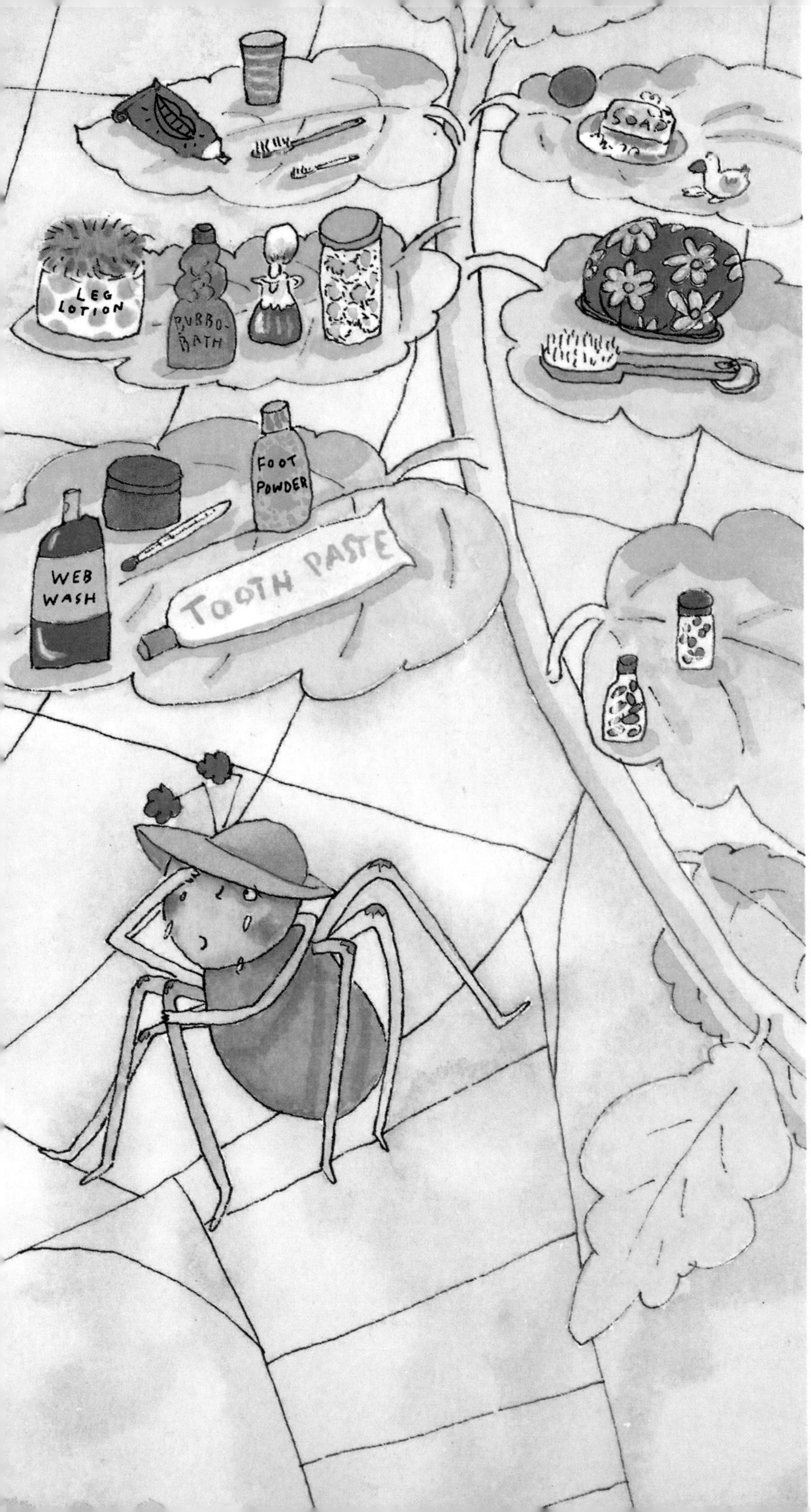

The eensy-weensy spider fell down and scraped her knees.
"Ouch!" cried the spider. "I need some Band-Aids, please!"
"How many?" asked her mama. "I only have a few."
Said the eensy-weensy spider, "Six of them will do."

The eensy-weensy spider fell *plop* into the brook.
"Help!" yelled the spider. "I forgot to look!"
"Reach!" called the beetle. "That's what you must do."
And the beetle lent the spider a helping leg or two.

SHOE SALE

The eensy-weensy spider went out to buy some shoes.
"Well," said her mama, "which ones will you choose?"
"Those," chose the spider, "the red ones over there."
Said her mama to the salesman, "We'd like to buy three pair."

The eensy-weensy spider went walking in the park.
Down went the sun. The park got very dark.
"Come!" squeaked the glowworm. "Follow me, I pray."
And the eensy-weensy spider went safely on her way.

The eensy-weensy spider had a heavy head.
"It's late!" said her mama. "Time to go to bed."
The spider was so tired she didn't make a peep,
And the eensy-weensy spider soon fell fast asleep.

The eensy-weensy spider slept right through the night.
When she awoke, the sun was shining bright.
"Good," said the spider, "there isn't any rain!"
And the eensy-weensy spider went up the spout again.